DEAR MOUSE FRIENDS, WELCOME TO THE

STONE AGE!

WELCOME TO THE STONE AGE . . . AND THE WORLD OF THE CAVEMICE!

CAPITAL: OLD MOUSE CITY

POPULATION: WE'RE NOT SURE. (MATH DOESN'T EXIST YET!) BUT BESIDES CAVEMICE, THERE ARE PLENTY OF DINOSAURS, <u>WAY</u> TOO MANY SABER-TOOTHED TIGERS, AND FEROCIOUS CAVE BEARS — BUT NO MOUSE HAS EVER HAD THE COURAGE TO COUNT THEM!

TYPICAL FOOD: PETRIFIED CHEESE SOUP

NATIONAL HOLIDAY: GREAT ZAP DAY, WHICH CELEBRATES THE DISCOVERY OF FIRE. RODENTS EXCHANGE GRILLED CHEESE SANDWICHES ON THIS HOLIDAY.

NATIONAL DRINK: MAMMOTH MILKSHAKES

CLIMATE: Unpredictable, WITH FREQUENT METEOR SHOWERS

cheese soup

milkshake

MONEY

SEASHELLS OF ALL SHAPES AND SIZES

MEASUREMENT

THE BASIC UNIT OF MEASUREMENT IS BASED ON THE LENGTH OF THE TAIL OF THE LEADER OF THE VILLAGE. A UNIT CAN BE DIVIDED INTO A HALF TAIL OR QUARTER TAIL. THE LEADER IS ALWAYS READY TO PRESENT HIS TAIL WHEN THERE IS A DISPUTE.

THE CAVEMICE

Geronimo

Trap

Thea

Benjamin

Bugsy Wugsy

Hercule Poirat

Grandma Ratrock

Geronimo Stilton

CAVEMICE

I'M A SCAREDY-MOUSE!

Scholastic Inc.

ISBN 978-0-545-74616-8

www.geronimostilton.com

Text by Geronimo Stilton
Original title *La tremenda carica dei tremendosauri*
Cover by Flavio Ferron
Illustrations by Giuseppe Facciotto (design) and Daniele Verzini (color)
Graphics by Marta Lorini and Yuko Egusa

Special thanks to Shannon Penney
Translated by Julia Heim
Interior design by Becky James

12 11 10 9 8 7 6 5 4 3 2 1   15 16 17 18 19 20/0

Printed in the U.S.A.   40
First printing, March 2015

MANY AGES AGO, ON PREHISTORIC MOUSE ISLAND, THERE
WAS A VILLAGE CALLED OLD MOUSE CITY. IT WAS INHABITED
BY BRAVE *RODENT SAPIENS* KNOWN AS THE CAVEMICE.
DANGERS SURROUNDED THE MICE AT EVERY TURN:
EARTHQUAKES, METEOR SHOWERS, FEROCIOUS DINOSAURS,
AND FIERCE GANGS OF SABER-TOOTHED TIGERS. BUT THE
BRAVE CAVEMICE FACED IT ALL WITH A SENSE OF HUMOR,
AND WERE ALWAYS READY TO LEND A HAND TO OTHERS.
HOW DO I KNOW THIS? I DISCOVERED AN
ANCIENT BOOK WRITTEN BY MY ANCESTOR, GERONIMO
STILTONOOT! HE CARVED HIS STORIES INTO STONE TABLETS
AND ILLUSTRATED THEM WITH HIS ETCHINGS.
I AM PROUD TO SHARE THESE STONE AGE STORIES WITH
YOU. THE EXCITING ADVENTURES OF THE CAVEMICE WILL
MAKE YOUR FUR STAND ON END, AND THE JOKES WILL
TICKLE YOUR WHISKERS! HAPPY READING!

Geronimo Stilton

WARNING! DON'T IMITATE THE CAVEMICE.
WE'RE NOT IN THE STONE AGE ANYMORE!

OUCH!

Ahhh, I love the beginning of summer! Trees are blooming, the sun is shining, the breeze ruffles your whiskers . . . how **peaceful**!

Even I, Geronimo Stiltonoot — the most COURAGEOUS journalist in all of prehistory (sort of!), the most tireless reporter in all of Old Mouse City (maybe!), the most famouse editor of *The Stone Gazette* (well, the **only** editor!) — decided to take a few days of vacation. Yes, that's right: I said vacation!

I rented a cute little STILT-HOUSE on the Rapidfire River. I couldn't wait to **RELAX** with my sister, Thea, and my sweet nephew Benjamin.

Once we arrived, I spent my time reading, drinking BIG CUPS of fern juice, and taking megalithic naps. Nothing could disturb this *dreamy* atmosph —

OooouUUUCh!

A Ballasaurus hit me square in the snout!

THE BALLASAURUS

The Ballasaurus is an armored reptile found only on prehistoric Mouse Island.

It is very playful! When it is in the mood for pranks, it rolls itself up into a ball, which is how it got its name. The Ballasaurus is a fairly lazy creature and doesn't like to stray far from home — so it is the only ball that voluntarily goes back into the hands of whoever threw it!

"BALLLLLLLLL!" a voice shouted as I rubbed my sore snout. What Paleozoic pain!

"Hey, Cousin! Get off the **BALLASAURUS** court!"

Oh, I almost forgot — my obnoxious cousin Trap had come with us, too. That mouse never misses a **vacation**!

"Do you really have to **play** right here?!" I squeaked.

"Where else would we play?" he scoffed, getting ready to throw again. "Come on, enough lounging around, lazybones! At this rate, by the end of the vacation you'll be even **flabbier** than before." He flexed his arms. "Look at me! Check out my abs and my bulging muscles."

Then Trap burst into a series of goofy poses, **spinning around** on his tail and making his stomach flop up and down

4

with the grace of a hippopotamosaur.

I was about to leave, but a wild yell made my fur stand on end.

"Woooooooooo!"

The noise was coming from . . . Trap, of course! He swung over my head, hanging on to a vine. He almost swiped my snout but then let go of the vine and cannonballed into the clear water of the Rapidfire River.

WOOOOOOOOO!

Careful!

SPLASHHHHHH!

A massive wave **soaked** me from the ends of my whiskers to the tip of my tail. Petrified provolone, I was wet!

"Not bad, huh?" Trap said, strutting out of the water and splashing all over me. "Am I an expert diver, or what?"

UGH!

Soaked and fed up, I decided to take a walk in the forest. I had to get away from the chaos, away from the splashing, and most of all, away from my cheese-brained cousin's bragging!

Grrr . . .

DRIP! DRIP! DRIP!

I headed into the thick **FOREST** and walked along the Rapidfire River until I found a perfect spot to rest.

A carpet of PiNe NeeDLeS covered the ground, blooming plants cooled the clearing, and best of all . . . no cannonballing cousin in sight! How **relaxing**!

I curled up in the shade of a prehistoric palm to take a nice nap. But before I could even close my eyes, a giant **SHADOW** covered the ground in front of me.

Gulp! What could it be?!

An Apatosaurus? A Megalosaurus? Or a **TERRIBLE** T-T-T-T. rex?! (Crusty cheese

rinds, just thinking about it makes my whiskers tremble in fright! I guess maybe I'm a bit of a scaredy-mouse.)

Quaking, I gulped and looked up. But it wasn't a dinosaur at all — it was just a **cloud** that had covered the sun. What a relief!

Then it started to rain . . .

Drip! Drip! Drip!

Ugh — it seems like every time I go on **vacation**, there's a rainstorm. And this was a real downpour!

DRIP DROP

DROP Ugh!

Drip Drip Drip
Drip
Drop Drip
Drop Drop

I had just **dried** off after Trap's cannonball, and now I was as soaked as a Paleozoic sponge. **HRUMPH!**

I was about to head back to the stilt-house, but the soggy sand had suddenly turned into disgusting **SLUDGE**.

I took one step and — **squish!** My paws were sucked down into the mud. Another step and — **GLUB!** I sank in the sludge up to my tail!

OOF! At this rate, it was going to take

Gulp!

Squissssssh!

forever to get back.

When I finally arrived at the stilt-house, I was dead tired and covered in gloppy **MUD**.

"**Helpppp!**" Trap exclaimed. "It's . . . it's . . . the Rapidfire River **monster**!"

"I'm not a monster!" I sighed. "It's me, you **CRAZY** mouse — it's Geronimo!"

I stumbled into the **STILT-HOUSE** to get out of the rain.

The river had risen quickly, and water **RUSHED** by faster than a mammoth

milkshake down Trap's throat. I had never seen anything like it — and we cavemice have seen our fair share of floods and **cat-astrophes**!

Suddenly, I noticed something in the rushing water.

"Look — it's a little **dinosaur**!" Thea cried.

Benjamin gasped. "And he seems to be in **trouble** . . ."

"Great rocky boulders!" I squeaked. "We have to do something!"

Eeeeek!

HEAVE-HO!

Bones and stones, this was **SERIOUS**!

I could see that the little (or not-so-little) dinosaur was a **baby** Tremendosaurus. He was flailing in the waves. The current was so strong that he could barely keep his head above water.

Now what?

"I don't know how long he can hold on!" Thea exclaimed.

"I have an **idea**," said Benjamin, lighting up. "Uncle Trap, pass me the **vine** that you were swinging on before."

"Huh?" Trap mumbled. That lazy rodent was half-asleep!

Luckily, Thea was QUICK on her paws. She jumped into the nearby pile of Trap's things — including a heap of blankets, bathing suits, and slices of Stinkerton, the most famouse and smelliest cheese in Old Mouse City. A moment later, she pulled out the vine that my cousin had used to swing between the trees. WHEW!

Thea ran to the riverbank and looped the vine around a tree trunk. While Trap, Benjamin, and I stood by, Thea threw the other end into the river toward the Tremendosaurus.

The baby dinosaur flailed about frantically and finally grabbed the vine with his teeth.

All we had to do now was PULL!

"HEAVE-HO! HEAVE-HO!"

Unfortunately, no matter how hard we pulled, we could move him only a few tail lengths. He was **SO HEAVY**!

But we couldn't give up.

"HEAVE-HOOOOOOO!"

The dinosaur did what he could, **thrashing** his feet and tail in the water, but nothing was working. At this rate, it would take a week to get him to shore!

"Trap!" Thea yelled. "Give a big **YANK** on the vine!"

But even Trap was having a Jurassically hard time.

"**HUFF, HUFF** ... **PANT, PANT** ..." he wheezed. "Fossilized feta, I just can't do it anymore!"

"I know what we need," Benjamin said suddenly. He sounded like he had his

PAWS on the answer!

He let go for a moment and yelled in Trap's ear as loudly as he could, "If you do this, we'll have **super-fondue** for dinner!"

Hearing those words, Trap seemed to regain all of his strength! The thought of a cheesy reward helped him give one last **POWERFUL** tug.

But as he did, the branch that was holding the vine **BROKE** with a snap! We were thrown to the ground. Thea landed on a pile of dried leaves, Benjamin and Trap ended up in the middle of a huge mud puddle, and I was thrown into a **THORNY** bush.

Bones and stones, it was prehistorically painful!

The good news was that, when we got back on our paws, we noticed that Trap's **SUPERPOWERFUL** tug had worked.

The baby dinosaur was standing right in front of our snouts!

He was shaking in fear and looking around, confused. Poor guy — he really seemed lost!

Huh?

A NAME FIT FOR A TREMENDOSAURUS

We were exhausted, SORE, and DRENCHED (and my tail was full of thorns!) — but we were happy. We'd saved the baby dinosaur!

The storm blew over, and the rain finally stopped. Benjamin went over to pet the Tremendosaurus's snout sweetly. "Are you okay, little guy?"

To answer his question, the DINO began to lick him happily. Then he

Ruff! Ruff!

Hey!

wagged his tail and bounded around licking us, too. How cute!

The sun came back out as quickly as it had gone.

The young Tremendosaurus STRETCHED and lay with his belly up to enjoy the weather. We WATCHED him closely — we were so curious about him!

"What is his name?"

"Where is his mom?"

"And his herd?"

Benjamin kneeled down close to the baby's snout and said slowly, "WHAT IS YOUR NAME?"

The Tremendosaurus jumped on his feet, let out a series of grunts, and then began to spin around and around and around.

We tried to guess his name . . .

"Spinner?"

"Whirlwind?"

"Swirly?"

But he shook his head at every guess. Rats!

Finally, Benjamin yelled, "CYCLONE!"

The little dinosaur began to whoop and stomp his FEET merrily. His name was Cyclone!

"My name is Benjamin," my nephew said, introducing himself with a smile. "Hello!"

Cyclone gave him a vigorous lick on the whiskers and began to grunt in his dinosaur language, twirling his tail curiously.

Thea, Trap, and I looked at one another, CONFUSED. We didn't understand a single bit of what he was saying!

But Benjamin seemed to understand everything perfectly. "Why don't you answer?" he urged us. "He asked you what your names are!"

"Oh, of course," I said, as mixed up as a mammoth milkshake. I introduced myself, and Thea and Trap.

CYCLONE

NAME: CYCLONE

SPECIES: *Tremendosaurus swirlium*

PERSONALITY: Extremely lively! He can never keep still. He can also make a tremendous mess!

WHAT HE EATS: He's an herbivore — he loves vegetables, apples, and prehistoric plums.

WHAT HE WON'T EAT: Prehistoric pizza or megalithic onion skewers

Cyclone responded with a wiggle, two shakes of his front right foot, and a small pirouette.

"He said that he fell in the river when he was playing, many tails away from here," Benjamin translated.

Then the dinosaur CRINKLED his neck, did two skips, and blew three super drooly raspberries.

"He said that usually he likes to play by himself, but . . ."

Cyclone wagged his tail four times.

"He's happy to have met us, and he would really like to stay with us!" Benjamin's eyes lit up. "Ohhh, Uncle, can we keep him?"

I shook my snout vigorously. It was one thing to help a baby dinosaur in trouble —

it was a whole different thing to adopt him forever!

But I wasn't prepared for the adorable, **begging** eyes of my favorite nephew. He was impossible to resist!

"Please, please, pleeeeaaaase!" Benjamin pleaded. "He's so sweet!"

Cyclone blew a raspberry on my face. "He's so POLITE!"

Cyclone let out a powerful belch. **BURRRRRP!**

"He's so, um, well-mannered . . ."

Cyclone crouched down and left me a gift: a **stinky** pile of dinosaur dung. Rat-munching rattlesnakes! I certainly didn't need a **SMELLY** mini-Tremendosaurus troublemaker to deal with!

As soon as Cyclone understood that I didn't have any intention of taking him with us, he **froze** immediately.

He was suddenly so calm. He approached me on tiptoe, batted his long eyelashes, and rubbed his snout against my shoulder, looking at me **pleadingly**.

Hmph . . . that really wasn't fair! Besides, I knew that Cyclone had his own dinosaur family somewhere that probably missed him. I tried to resist . . .

"Well, maybe we can take him in for just a little while, until . . ."

I didn't even have time to finish my sentence before Benjamin and Cyclone **JUMPED** on me and covered me with hugs, tickles, licks on the snout, megalithic pats on the back, and happy tail thwacks!

OOF! I could hardly move!

Thea and Trap cried,

"HOORAY, CYCLONE!"

A CYCLONE INDEED!

Benjamin and Cyclone got along really well. They were **best friends** in no time at all!

And we immediately understood where the baby dinosaur got his name. He was a real CYCLONE — no, a hurricane — no, a cat-astrophe! First of all, Cyclone

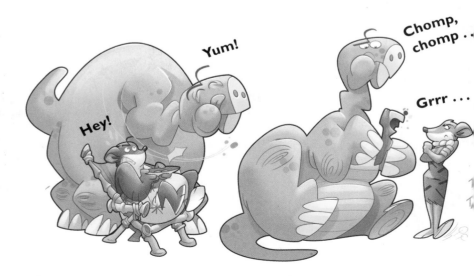

Hey!

Yum!

Chomp, chomp . .

Grrr . . .

couldn't keep still for a second.

He munched on everything he could munch on, **chomped** on everything he could chomp on, and DROOLED all over everything he could drool on. Basically, he was a prehistoric calamity!

"Maybe he needs to play more," Trap guessed, as the little (or not-so-little) guy SCARFED DOWN the last bit of cheesy fondue left in the stilt-house.

High five!

"So let's PLAY, then!" I squeaked, exasperated.

In no time, Thea and Trap created a Stone Age racquetball court and invited Cyclone to play. (I decided it was safer to stay on the sidelines and watch. You might say I'm a scaredy-mouse, but I'm just too fond of my tail!) The game was a good idea, but none of us had any idea how POWERFUL Cyclone was. Holding the

SHOOOOOOOOOOOM!

racquet with his tail, he was able to smack the **BALL** out of sight!

"Careful, Geronimo!" Thea exclaimed.

I looked up to see the ball *FLYING* toward me.

"WHOOOOAAA!"

I yelled, trying to leap out of the way.

But the ball hit me straight on. Rats! A

Heeeeeelp!

BUMP as big as a monolith* popped up right in the middle of my forehead. I was in a daze, so I couldn't move out of the way — and another ball flew right at me!

Finally, Thea jumped

SHOOOOOOMM!

SHOOOOOOMM!

SHOOOOOOMM!

on the baby dinosaur's back to **STOP** him. "That's enough!" she cried.

PREHISTO-NOTE
*A monolith is an enormouse prehistoric monument planted in the ground; usually a tall, narrow stone

Cyclone was not happy about my sister's interruption. He was having too much FUN playing!

Frustrated, he began to wiggle and squirm and ROMP back and forth with Thea still on his back.

"Cyclone!" Thea yelled. "We aren't at the Dino Rodeo! STOP!"

Trap could have used his massive muscles to hold down the dinosaur's head, but even he was running away along the riverbank, breathless.

I really couldn't take it anymore. All the confusion was making my snout shake!

But if that WILD little guy thought he was going to ruin my vacation, he was wrong. For all the thorns on a cactus, I wasn't going to let that happen!

YOU WANTED A VACATION, STILTONOOT?

Quiet as a mouse, I snuck away and settled under the **shade** of a big Paleozoic apple tree. Then I decided to **climb** it. I wanted to get far away from any more Cyclonic surprises!

Well, *climb* isn't really the right word, since I **suffer** from a teeny-weeny, super-mini fear of **heights**. Some might even call me a scaredy-mouse. So I chose a branch that was fairly low down — okay, practically on the ground — and I got comfortable. **AAAHH!**

Wasn't this supposed to be a **relaxing** vacation?

I tried to forget my troubles by taking a little nap. I **dreamed** that I was in a huge tub filled with **cheesy fondue**! I was just about to eat a mouthful of Jurassic Jack cheese when —

"**No!**"

I jumped. What was that?

"**I SAID No!**"

I opened my eyes and saw Benjamin nearby, lecturing Cyclone. But the little dinosaur wasn't listening. Instead, he ran under my tree and began **HEAD-BUTTING** it to make fruit fall off the branches!

Cheese and crackers — I guess Benjamin's

Listen!

lecture hadn't worked!

I was suddenly bombarded with a shower of giant falling apples . . .

BONK! BONK! BONK!

. . . right before the tree trunk gave out and **CRACKED** with a mega-massive slam.

SMAAAASSSHHH!

WHOOOOOOOOOOA!

When my snout stopped spinning, I looked around and could hardly believe my eyes.

Great rocky boulders, Cyclone had caused a **megalithic** mess!

SO MUCH FOR RELAXING!

We looked around at the **destruction** Cyclone had caused along the river. Petrified cheese, the place was a wreck! Trees had been uprooted, plants and branches were **scattered** all over the ground, and even a wall of the stilt-house had been knocked down.

"Stiltonoot, what is this?! I leave you at my peaceful oasis by the river, and now it looks like a **battlefield**! I demand an explanation!"

Oh, rats! It was Theo

Thunderclap, the grumpy OWNER of the stilt-house we had rented for our vacation.

He hollered so loudly that Cyclone huddled in a corner behind Benjamin, whining and bowing his long neck in shame. Finally, he was standing still for a minute!

Watching the little guy cower, I couldn't help feeling bad. Yes, Cyclone was responsible for the disaster — but then again, he was a very young dinosaur! Thunderclap seemed so threatening that I didn't want to make him mad at our little Tremendosaurus. Who knew what kind of terrible PUNISHMENT Thunderclap might give him!

I tried to come up with another reason for the mess. "Umm, well, Mister Thunderclap, you see . . . the **rain** . . ."

It was no use. He glared at me.

"The wind . . ." I muttered.

He furrowed his eyebrows.

"The . . . um, the humidity . . ."

"That's enough jabbering, Stiltonoot!" Thunderclap burst out. "I don't know exactly what happened here, but you need to repay me for all the **damages**!"

"Oh, we'll fix everything, we promise," Thea said quickly.

Trap agreed. "And we'll repay you. That is, he" — he said, pointing at me — "he will REPAY you for all the damages, shell for shell!"

Thunderclap glowered. "By tonight, I want all of this to look like new. Plus, you owe me one hundred shells to reimburse me for my trouble. And, most important — I want you all far away from here by nightfall!" THUNDERCLAP concluded, stomping away.

So we got to work. We replanted the trees, fixed the STILT-HOUSE, tidied up the grounds, and gathered all the apples that had fallen from the tree. At sunset, exhausted, we left for Old Mouse City. By the time we passed the city wall, it was already dark!

Zzzzzz ...

Yawn!

EITHER HIM . . . OR YOU!

I thought that our TROUBLES were finally over, but little did I know how wrong I was!

Once we arrived in the city, Thea and Trap went home. I was alone with Cyclone and Benjamin in my cave — or, I should say, OUTSIDE my cave. Cyclone took up so much space that I couldn't fit inside!

Before I could do anything, my exhausted nephew curled up next to the baby Tremendosaurus and immediately fell asleep, right at the entrance to the cave.

And Cyclone, who normally had so much wild energy, yawned and curled his neck protectively around his new friend. Fossilized feta, they were so *sweet*!

With a sigh, I covered them with a blanket, gave Benjamin a good-night **kiss**, and even gave a PECK to the little dinosaur, too.

What can I say? My heart is as soft as a prehistoric pot of fondue!

The next morning, the sun was already high in the sky by the time I woke up. I jolted to my paws as the CRIES of

Good night!

Gossip Radio rang through the air. Bones and stones, what a racket!

Speeeeeciaaaaal editiooooooon!

In case you don't know, Gossip Radio is the **LEAST TRUSTWORTHY** news source of the whole Stone Age. It's run by my ARCHENEMY, Sally Rockmousen, and never broadcasts anything true. It **DISTORTS** all the information and transforms it into a crazy, sensational scoop. And this time . . .

"SPEEEEECIAAAAAL EDITIOOOOOOOON! AN EXTREMELY FEROCIOUS TREMENDOSAURUS IS ATTACKING OLD MOUSE CITY!"

one of Sally's pterodactyls squawked.

Double-twisted rat tails! What?!

There was more.

"DANGER OF EXTINCTION FOR ALL
PREHISTORIC MICE!"

I jumped to my paws. Hang on a minute . . .

I **turned toward** the cave and —
rats! Just as I feared, Cyclone and Benjamin
weren't in the entrance anymore. They
weren't **anywhere** in sight. Instead,
from my cave all the way to Singing Rock
Square, the city was one enormouse,
uninterrupted **disaster** area. Uprooted
trees, missing doors, torn-up roads full of
HOLES and deep craters . . .

And, of course, all of that chaos looked
awfully familiar. It could only have been
caused by a small (or not-so-small) **WILD**
Tremendosaurus!

I found Thea standing near the wall at the edge of Old Mouse City. She stared at me in disbelief, shaking her head.

Cyclone had passed by there, too, and our wall (which was supposed to defend the city against outside attacks) was **nibbled** at, **broken**, CRACKED, and completely demolished in places!

"Geronimo Stiltonoot!" a voice thundered. Pointy Triceratops horns, what now?

The voice belonged to Ernest Heftymouse, the village leader. I had never seen him so exasperated! His cheeks were red, and his eyes were bugging out of his snout.

"What is all this, Stiltonoot?!" he barked. "There is a destructive Tremendosaurus scampering around Old Mouse City with your nephew!"

"Well . . ." I said, trying to make myself

really, really small, like the teeny-tiny fleas that lived on my fur coat. "Okay, let's say that they're acquaintances. But they don't know each other very well. HARDLY AT ALL!"

"Oh, really?" Heftymouse **scowled**, unconvinced. "Well, do you know what those two are up to?"

"Um . . ." I muttered. "Are they doing their homework?"

Ernest Heftymouse hollered, **"THEY'RE DESTROYING OLD MOUSE CITY!"**

Stiltonoot!

Um . . .

My tail was in a twist. And then it got worse, because a herd

49

of angry Old Mouse City citizens had just approached.

"That beast destroyed my hanging garden!"

"He gobbled up all my bean reserves for next year!"

"He is a **calamity** of megalithic proportions!"

"You need to stop him, Stiltonoot!" Heftymouse said firmly. "You have until tomorrow to get him out of here. If you can't, you will be the one *KICKED OUT* of Old Mouse City. It's either him . . . or you!"

Oh, for the love of all things cheesy! This was a DISASTER. How was I going to tell Benjamin that Cyclone had to go? But most important — where **were** Benjamin and Cyclone?

"Let's look for them at the port," suggested Thea.

Down by the water, rays of sunshine cast a golden waterfall of light over Old Mouse City. We could see the shadows of two figures (a small one and a GIANT one) on the dock. Was it them?

HE MISSES HIS HOME!

As soon as Thea and I called their names, Benjamin **RAN** to meet us, looking relieved. But **CYCLONE** stayed curled up on the edge of the dock, staring at the horizon. He seemed **sad**.

Thea narrowed her eyes at Benjamin and squeaked, "Do you know how worried we were? Not only did you **destroy** half of Old Mouse City, but then you **disappeared** without apologizing!"

While Benjamin hung his snout, I walked over to Cyclone. "What's the matter?"

The Tremendosaurus let out an unhappy **sigh**. Not even his tail twitched. Benjamin walked up to him and **stroked** his neck. "He misses his home!" he explained. "That's part of the reason why he was so **ROWDY** — he didn't mean to destroy Old Mouse City. He just isn't used to the city! He was born and raised in a much **wilder** place."

Just then, Cyclone let out an enormouse **CRY**.

SiGH

He misses his home!

"WAAAAAAAAAAAAHHH!"

His giant tears flowed freely. In a few minutes, we were all completely soaked by them!

"He doesn't want to tell me why he left his herd," Benjamin continued sadly. "But now he misses his family!"

"Poor little guy!" Thea exclaimed. Then she whispered something in my ear. "Pssst psst psssst . . ."

But she was speaking too softly, and I couldn't understand her.

"What?"

She came even closer. "Psssst psst . . ."

"WHAAAAT?" I cried. "Squeak louder. I can't hear you!"

Impatient, Thea took me by the ear and PULLED me aside.

"Ouch!" I yelped.

"Do you have cheese in your ears?" she said. "I was saying that this would be a good time to get Cyclone out of the city without hurting Benjamin's feelings too much!"

Of course! Thea was absolutely right. But doing what she said meant that . . .

"EXACTLY!" Thea said, reading my mind. "We have to take Cyclone to find his family!"

Bones and stones! A few mice searching for a herd of Tremendosauruses in the middle of who knows where? That sounded like a PREHISTORIC DISASTER waiting to happen!

"Umm . . . well, actually, I . . ." I muttered hesitantly.

"Uncle Geronimo!" Benjamin called,

turning toward me with wide eyes. "I wanted to ask you if . . . maybe . . ."

"Of course!" Thea answered for me with a wink. "We're off to find the Tremendosauruses!"

My nephew jumped up and threw his arms around my neck. "HOORAY! You're the most mouserific uncle in all of the prehistoric world!"

I thought he was being a little too optimistic about my ability

Um···

Thanks!

to track down a pack of dangerous dinosaurs, but I decided not to squeak that out loud for now.

I also couldn't help thinking that I really would have rather been sleeping! I really am a scaredy-mouse . . .

Trap couldn't come with us this time because his business partner, Greasella Stonyfur, needed his help cleaning up the Rotten Tooth Tavern. The night before, they'd had a SPICY SLOP COOKING FESTIVAL — which was as sloppy as it sounds!

So Thea, Benjamin, Cyclone, and I headed out on our MiSSiON. We were taking the baby dinosaur back to his herd!

ROOOOAAAARRRR!

A few steps from the city I was already **huffing** and puffing worse than the Great Gurgling Geyser. How epically exhausting!

Every time Cyclone saw a tree, he ran with all his might and . . . **BONK!** He bashed his head against the tree trunks to make the fruit fall. Then he gobbled up all the fruit in one bite. Jurassic **PEACHES** and **COCONUTS** disappeared in seconds!

I couldn't help giggling as I watched the little Tremendosaurus having *fun* with the peaches. He **spit** the pits out happily, wagging his tail and laughing in delight.

After we'd been walking for a while, a cry startled us.

"AAAAYYYAAA!"

Who was that?! The voice seemed to be coming from the top of a tall Paleozoic plum **tree** that Cyclone had his eye on. Without noticing, Cyclone started head-butting the tree, until . . .

THUNK! THUNK!

Whoaaaaa!

Two **LARGE**, **furry**, and **FANGED** bodies fell to the ground!

Thea, Benjamin, and I were PARALYZED with fright. The two lumps were actually two saber-toothed tigers from Tiger Khan's band of fearsome felines. Yikes! They were the **fiercest** enemies of us cavemice!

Luckily, we were still far away and had time to duck behind a bush.

Cyclone didn't have much to fear, though. He was much **bigger** than the two felines! He looked at them threateningly.

When the tigers noticed that there was a Tremendosaurus in front of them, they JUMPED like they had just landed on a thornbush.

"G-g-good morning," the first one stammered to Cyclone, **shaking** like a leaf. "E-e-enjoy your food!"

"I-i-if you don't mind, we'll just get out of your WaY," the second tiger continued, forcing a smile. "These plums are certainly much tastier than we are!"

Then they darted away, *FASTER* than a Velociraptor.

Benjamin cheered. "Way to go, Cyclone!"

But Thea and I weren't feeling very calm. What were two members of the Saber-Toothed Squad doing in that tree? And where was the rest of their gang? I didn't want to find out!

G-good morning...

Gulp!

THE SCRITCH-SCRATCH FOREST

We didn't know exactly where Cyclone's herd was, so we walked along the edge of the Rapidfire River until we **stumbled upon** a cluster of really old trees.

"According to my calculations, this should be the Scritch-Scratch Forest," Thea announced.

We looked around cautiously. The FOREST was thick and green, yet there was something strange about it. The trees seemed to have thousands of little **EYES** that were spying on us from behind the leaves!

"Do you hear that?" Thea whispered.

Benjamin and I **PERKED UP** our ears.

"It's some kind of buzzing," I whispered.

But I couldn't say anything else before a swarm of prehistoric Bees flew out of a hole in a nearby tree! I felt their stingers sink into my fur. Youch!

But the strangest thing of all is that they TALKED to us!

"Bzzzzzz . . . these woods are oursssss!"

"Bzzzzzz . . . rodents, get ouuuutttt!"

We had never seen or heard anything like it!

63

But we were afraid of the bees, and we darted away with our paws up until we found a clearing. Satisfied, the insects went away as quickly as they had appeared.

We were safe, but now we were covered with **stings** — and they itched like crazy! It was impossible not to scratch.

SCRITCH   SCRITCH
    SCRATCH   SCRATCH

And then I realized — that's why the forest was named Scritch-Scratch!

When the itchiness finally died down, a swarm of hornets **DARTED** out of a nearby honeycomb and headed right for us. We were petrified — we really couldn't catch a break!

Those tiny beasts spotted us, and . . . ZIP! They headed right for us. Youuuuch!

Finally, huffing and puffing and covered with stings, we **escaped** from the hornets' clearing.

Since the sun was setting, Thea suggested that we set up camp in a safe spot.

Cyclone **wagged** his tail in approval. (He had also wolfed down a bunch of Paleozoic plums and his belly was gurgling, so he couldn't sit still!)

"I think I'll take these," Benjamin said to him, grabbing the remaining plums. "I'll give them to you slowly. You can't just gorge yourself like that!"

I smiled. My nephew was so sweet and responsible with that little dinosaur!

DON'T MAKE ME SUFFER ANYMORE!

As the sun sank in the sky, we hurried to set up our tents.

Great rocky boulders, I could have slept for a whole GEOLOGICAL ERA!

But just as soon as we said good night and I closed my eyes, a screeching song made us all JUMP.

"Youuuu ... you stole my heeeaaart ... don't ever leaaaave!"

Holey cheese, I had never heard anyone so tone-deaf!

From her tent, Thea hollered, "Ugh, Geronimo, can't you sing tomorrow morning?"

"But that's not me!" I replied, offended. "There's someone out there who's an even WORSE singer than I am!"

I clapped my paws over my ears as the serenade continued. "Don't make me suuuuuffer anymore . . . Come baaaack, don't gooooo!"

We poked our snouts out of our tents — and suddenly it all made sense.

Lit by the moonlight, several mosquitoes as big as coconuts were buzzing around, **singing** their greatest hits.

I jumped as high as a ball of bouncing mozzarella. "Those are Prehistoric Musical Mosquitoes! They sing their songs, and if they don't get enough applause, they **BITE** everyone in sight!"

So we had no choice! Even though we desperately wanted to go to sleep, we had to listen to that **TERRIBLE** concert.

And in the end, so we wouldn't get bitten, Thea, Benjamin, and I applauded so loudly that the mosquitoes decided to do an encore!

PETRIFIED PROVOLONE, WHAT A NIGHTMARE!

ATTACK OF THE FLUFFY BISON

The next morning, we left the Scritch-Scratch Forest and headed on to the Rumbling Plain in **SEARCH** of Cyclone's herd.

There were no Tremendosauruses in sight — but we could see a **dark** and **THREATENING** cloud off in the distance. Fossilized feta, could it be another downpour? As I looked closer, it didn't seem like a **storm cloud**. It seemed more like a . . .

"That's a herd of **FLUFFY BISON**!" Thea yelled. "They're headed right for us — quick, we have to find a safe place to hide!"

Fluffy bison are just like traditional **PREHISTORIC** bison, except that they have supersoft, curly, long fur that hangs all the way to the ground. Basically, they look like they're covered with **cotton balls**!

Even though they look soft and fuzzy, they are very DANGEROUS animals. They're always ANGRY — especially when they see intruders on their land!

Thea was right! A gang of fluffy bison were heading our way — and they were moving

TRADITIONAL PREHISTORIC BISON

FLUFFY BISON

FAST. They were just a few tails away from us, and there was nowhere to hide! They would arrive in **ten** . . . **nine** . . . **eight** . . .

But just when it seemed like we were going to be smashed as flat as prehistoric pancakes, Thea came up with a **fabumouse** idea.

She waited until the first bison passed close to us. Then she jumped up and landed right on his back! The bison didn't notice a thing — he was too busy *CHARGING*. Benjamin, following Thea's lead, did the same thing. Now it was my turn . . .

Shaking from the ends of my ears to the tip of my tail, I closed my eyes and **JUMPED** with all my might!

WAS I ABOUT TO BECOME EXTINCT?

WHAT DID HE SAY?!

When I opened my eyes, I was still alive —
and I was riding on Cyclone!

That's right! The little (or not-so-little)
Tremendosaurus had wrapped himself in
our blankets to hide among the bison. Then
he had run to my rescue, scooping me up
onto his back. He was my dino hero!

The only problem was that I was sitting
BACKWARD — my back was turned toward
the dinosaur's head and my PAWS
were facing his long tail. Cyclone ran and
jumped merrily across the field, giving me
a terrible tummyache! Oh, my snout
was spinning!

When the bison ran on and the dinosaur finally **STOPPED**, I climbed down from Cyclone's back. It felt like my tail was where my whiskers should be and my ears were where my paws should be. My stomach was all twisted up like a strip of Stone Age string cheese. **BLURP!**

Thea and Benjamin had jumped off their **dangerous** rides, too, and they caught up with us at the river's edge. There, we spotted an old rodent enjoying the shade of a sequoia tree.

"Oh, for all the thorns on a cactus!" he squeaked. "I've seen **MICE** ride

Trottosauruses and fly on Puffasauruses — but mice who ride BISON? That is really something!"

The old rodent climbed to his paws and walked slowly over to meet us. He had dark, ruffled fur and a nose as red as a primordial pepper.

"However," he continued with a scowl, "what is all this RUCKUS? First the Tremendosauruses down on the other riverbank . . . then rodents riding bison . . . A mouse really just can't get a moment's peace around here anymore!"

Thea, Benjamin, and I stared at him with our mouths hanging open.

"What did you say?!" Benjamin stammered. "Did you say that there are TREMENDOSAURUSES on the other riverbank?"

78

Our search for Cyclone's herd was over!
Thea was so thrilled that she planted a
kiss right on the old rodent's snout. His
surprise froze him up like a GLACIER!
But we couldn't explain to him why we were
so happy. There was no **time** to waste.
We had to get across the river!

TREMENDOSAURUS VALLEY

It was going to be tougher than we thought to cross the river, because Cyclone didn't want to wade across. He was still **frightened** of the water! I understood how he felt. After all, I'm a scaredy-mouse myself!

"Be BRAVE, Cyclone — we're here with you," Benjamin encouraged him.

"Plus, your **mom** is on the other side!" Thea added.

"And look how **calm** the river is," I said with a big, fake smile. The river was actually full of rapids, but it didn't seem like the time to point that out. "Umm . . . it really reminds me of a relaxing **hot spring**!"

It was no use. Cyclone wouldn't budge! He just stood there with his tremendous feet planted **FIRMLY** in the sand.

We were about to give up when Benjamin had a **fabumouse** idea.

Nonchalantly, he pulled out one of those giant plums and began to **play** with it right in front of Cyclone.

The dinosaur gulped and began to **DROOL**. He took a tiny half-tail step toward the fruit. The plan was working!

Benjamin **tossed** the plum to Thea. She **THREW** the plum to me. And I **lobbed** it back to Benjamin.

So we kept at it!

Yum!

Toss after toss, without noticing, Cyclone stepped *CLOSER* to the edge of the river. Then he put one **FOOT** in the water, then the other, and so on, until . . .

HOP! Cyclone jumped into the water.

At that point, Benjamin THREW the plum to the opposite shore.

Cyclone hadn't taken his eyes off the fruit, and he didn't notice that he had walked into the water. In fact, he didn't even seem to notice when he **waded** all the way across!

Good job, Cyclone!

Soon he was on the other bank, SOAKING WET but satisfied, with the giant plum in his mouth.

At that point, I pulled Benjamin close. Together, we swam across the river. MISSION ACCOMPLISHED!

Cyclone finished his plum and peered around. He sniffed here and there, and wagged his tail excitedly. He seemed to recognize this place!

Then he darted off as quickly as a LIGHTNING BOLT, as if he knew exactly where he was going!

We followed him as fast as our paws would take us, through the heart of the FOREST. Eventually, we ended up in a grassy space that overlooked an enormouse valley.

The valley below was an amazing place, surrounded by rocks that had been chiseled and polished by the wind. But it also looked chaotic. Trees were uprooted, bushes were trampled, and the ground was covered with leftover scraps of fruit.

We'd found TREMENDOSAURUS VALLEY!

Benjamin gasped. "That's why Cyclone destroys everything — he's just copying his herd!"

My nephew was RIGHT. Yet there was something that didn't make sense. If this was Tremendosaurus Valley, where were the Tremendosauruses?

"Maybe the herd moved to look for Cyclone," Thea suggested.

Just then, Benjamin pointed. "Look, over

there is a trail of CRUMBLED rocks!"

"But Old Mouse City is that way," I said.

Great rocky boulders, we needed to **follow** the herd before they accidentally destroyed our city!

Luckily, it wasn't hard to track Cyclone's relatives. Their **PRINTS** were so big that following them was as easy as sniffing out **STINKY** cheese!

Plus, Cyclone was moving very fast. He couldn't wait to find his parents. When our

paws got too **tired**, he let us ride on his back and **rest** while he kept running.

As night fell, Cyclone continued on, step by step. He was **tireless**! By the time dawn broke, we could already see Old Mouse City.

Suddenly, Cyclone began to run even **faster**. He had spotted his herd!

WE'RE FRIENDS!

Cyclone's herd was huge — in fact, it was tremendous! There were **BiG** dinosaurs and **small** dinosaurs, some as **TALL** as mountains or as **short** as hills. But all of them — and I mean all of them — looked at us **THREATENINGLY**!

Yikes!

Eeeek, eeeek?!

A horrible thought crossed my mind: Maybe they thought that we had **KIDNAPPED** Cyclone! Yikes! Luckily, our friend began

Grrr . . .

Grunt!

to **GRUNT** and wiggle, moving his neck **UP** and **DOWN** as if he was explaining something.

"He's telling them that we saved him from the river," said Benjamin, translating for us.

At that point, a **giant** pink Tremendosaurus stepped out of the herd

and peered at us carefully. She was big and looked angry — and made my whiskers wobble with **fright**!

"We're friends — **friends**!" I yelled.

The dinosaur approached, looking closely at Cyclone. Then she stroked his tail and licked his head.

It was Cyclone's mom!

After they'd reunited, she planted herself in front of us, bent her neck down, and looked us right in the **EYES**. Oh, rats — this wasn't good!

I squeezed my eyes shut, preparing for premature EXTINCTION. But, surprisingly, the beast's scowl turned into the sweetest smile I had ever seen! The mama Tremendosaurus licked us all with lots of slobber to say thank you, and went back to explain the situation to the rest of the herd.

Hearing the news that Cyclone was back, the Tremendosauruses began to JUMP, dance, stomp their feet, and do somersaults and twirls to celebrate.

Petrified cheese! Their celebration was going to completely destroy Old Mouse City!

All of a sudden, Cyclone's mom stopped. She seemed WORRIED. She said something to the other members of the herd, and they stopped, too. Then she gestured with her snout and invited me to CLIMB on her head!

I decided to do as she asked. It didn't seem like a good idea to say no to her — after all, she could have turned me into a prehistoric pancake with one STOMP!

TIGERS ON THE HORIZON!

Holding tight to Cyclone's mom as I sat way, way, wayyyy above the ground, I noticed something very *alarming*. There were a few figures trying to slip through a narrow passage in the **CITY WALL**, which was still a crumbly mess from Cyclone's rampage a few days earlier. I

Oh no!

squinted to see better — and almost fell off the Tremendosaurus's back!

It was Tiger Khan and his SABER-TOOTHED SQUAD!

Now I understood why the tigers had been up in the tree two days before. They must have been the Squad's **LOOKOUTS**, sent ahead by their leader. What a megalithic mess!

"**TIGERS ON THE HORIZON!**" I yelled with all my might.

Roar!

But Benjamin and Thea couldn't hear me in all that confusion. I was forced to hold myself steady with one **PAW** so I could wave and point with the other. "Old Mouse City is being attacked by **TIGER KHAN**!"

"Yes!" Thea yelled back with a grin. "Cyclone's mother is as graceful as a **swan**!"

Moldy mozzarella, they didn't understand a thing I'd said!

At that moment, my paw lost its grip. I began to **slip** down the Tremendosaurus's neck **FASTER** and **FASTER** and **FASTER**. I clapped my paw over my eyes. I couldn't watch! I was about to reach her tail, and after that I would be **smashed** to the ground!

I prepared myself for the worst . . . but nothing happened. Instead, it suddenly felt like I was going **UP** instead of down!

When I opened my eyes, I understood what had happened. The dinosaur had lifted up her tail just in time to launch me into the air — and now I was flying through the sky! **WHOOOOOOaaaaaa!**

If that wasn't bad enough, I was headed right for the saber-toothed tigers. I was going to be a mouse-meat sandwich!

After soaring and tumbling through the air, I landed right on top of Tiger Khan. Oof! There was no mistaking him. He always stank like the sludge of

H-h-hello!

Looky here . . .

the terrible Stinky Swamp!

"Argh! Since when do **Flying rats** exist?" one of the tigers near him spat.

Tiger Khan grabbed me by the scruff of the neck and **dragged** me right up to his scowling face. "And where did you come from? Hmm — haven't I seen you somewhere before?"

Shaking like a giant fern, I was about to **mutter** my last words when Tiger Khan spotted something behind me. He turned as **white** as a slab of mozzarella.

I turned, too — and couldn't believe my eyes.

The Tremendosauruses were **COMING** right for the Saber-Toothed Squad, with Cyclone in the lead!

TREMENDOSAURUS REVENGE!

There is nothing — and I mean nothing — that scares saber-toothed tigers more than Tremendosauruses on the charge. And that's not surprising — even one step from baby Cyclone would squash them as FLAT as a slice of prehistoric provolone!

The Tremendosauruses *ran* right at the Saber-Toothed Squad, as determined as ever. Cyclone's mom grabbed some of the no-longer-so-fearsome felines and began to TOSS them in the air like pebbles. Another dinosaur grabbed a tiger by his tail and used his SUPERSHARP saber-teeth to scratch his back. One female

Tremendosaurus even picked a group of tigers and used them as curlers to curl her tail!

At the sight of the charging beasts, the other tigers scattered. Some of them slipped, some lost their balance, some hid as best they could . . .

But nothing could stop the amazing Tremendosauruses! They overpowered the felines like they were tiny ants, and tossed them far away.

I had never seen tigers look so terrified! There was no hope for those nasty fanged felines.

Hee, hee!

GULP

GRT GRT

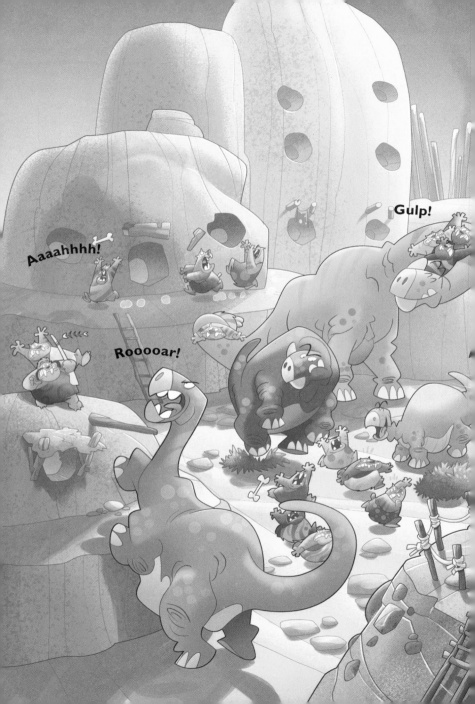

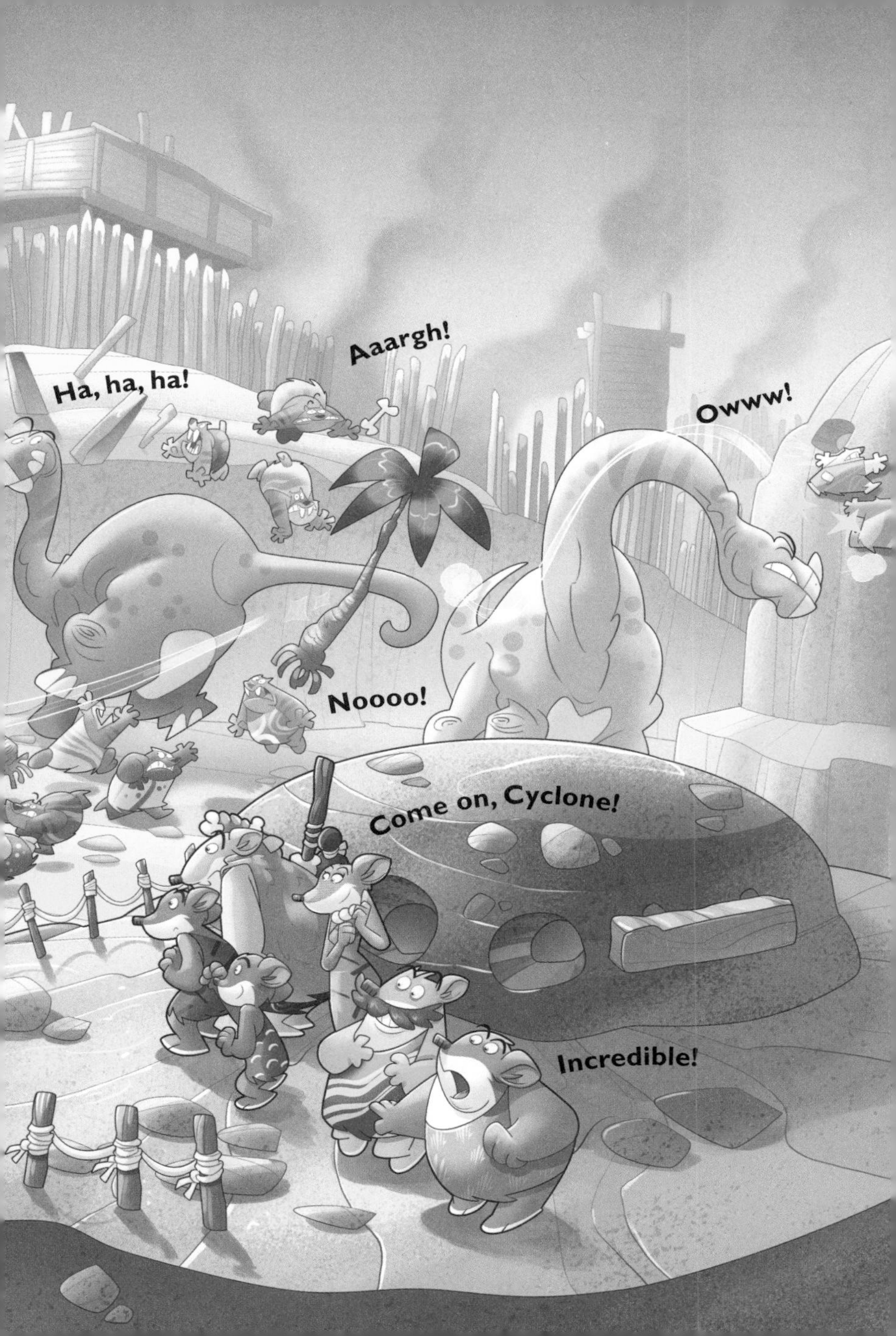
Ha, ha, ha!
Aaargh!
Owww!
Noooo!
Come on, Cyclone!
Incredible!

The battle was **OVER** before it began!

Even Tiger Khan, who wasn't the brightest star in the sky, knew that the tigers **didn't stand a chance** against the dinosaurs.

Purple with rage, he cupped his big paws around his fangs and yelled with all his might, "**RETREAT!** Go back to Bugville, my brave companions! I just remembered

I have . . . ummm . . . I have an urgent **THING** to do there today!"

And so the tigers fled, exhausted and covered with bruises.

We all ran over to **hug** Cyclone. Old Mouse City was saved!

VICTORY!

GOOD-BYE, BIG GUYS!

The citizens of Old Mouse City poured out from behind the wall to celebrate the Tremendosauruses' victory. They had saved our city! And the beasts celebrated the only way they knew how, of course — they began to **RUN** and **JUMP** boisterously in and out of the city, causing panic and destruction!

They **CRUMBLED** the remaining pieces of the wall, demolished dozens of huts, **tore down** all the trees, and crushed whatever was crushable.

Thundering Tremendosaurus feet, **what a mess**!

ERNEST HEFTYMOUSE, the head of the village, was beside himself. "Stiltonoot! You again! What is going on here?! A raid by the Saber-Toothed Squad might have been better than this!"

At that moment, a **HUGE ROCK** fell off a nearby roof and hit him right on the snout.

BONK!

Thea and Benjamin began **DEFENDING** the herd. "Try to understand them!" Benjamin explained. "The Tremendosauruses have some **WILD** habits, but that's only because they're used to living freely in open spaces!"

107

"Plus, it isn't easy to *move* around in a city at their size," Thea added. With a wink, she continued, "After all, you know what it's like to be **BIGGER AND STRONGER** than everyone else, right?"

What?!

Heftymouse blushed. "Well, yes, I suppose I do." Then he remembered that he was supposed to be **ANGRY**. "But what does my superior mousely strength have to do with these destructive beasts?!"

Just then, an **IRRITATED** Tremendosaurus headed his way. Suddenly, the head of the village changed his tone!

"No, no, I didn't mean beasts — I meant sweet, delicate creatures . . . who are so lovely, and such beautiful, superchic colors!"

108

The dinosaur huffed, unconvinced, but headed back to the rest of the herd.

"The good news," Benjamin said, "is that our friend Cyclone offered to teach his herd some good manners . . ."

"And the Tremendosauruses have all volunteered to help **repair** the wall and the destroyed houses!" Thea added.

Heftymouse raised an eyebrow. "Well, by the Great Zap, that is good news!"

And in just a few hours, thanks to the **hard work** of the Tremendosauruses, the wall was back in place, the huts were repaired, and the trees were replanted. Old Mouse City was good as new!

It was time for our enormouse friends to head home. Trap had finished cleaning his tavern by then and could come and say **good-bye** to Cyclone.

The little dinosaur licked our faces one by one, then gently hugged Benjamin with his tail. Cyclone shook his big head with emotion.

"Me, too," said Benjamin, drying his tears. "I will never forget you!"

Then the dinosaur romped over to his mom, and the herd began their JOURNEY back to their valley.

"Well, I have to say that I'm going to miss

Have a good trip!

Bye!

that **troublemaker** a little bit," I admitted, feeling sad to see him go.

"Me, too!" Benjamin said with a sigh as he watched the Tremendosauruses **TREK** into the distance.

And so, dear friends, with a bit of sadness (but also some relief!), our STRANGE ADVENTURE with the most hotheaded, wild — and helpful! — Tremendosaurus of the prehistoric world came to an end.

Even though I may be a bit of a scaredy-mouse, I promise I'll be ready for my next adventure in the Stone Age, or I'm not . . .

Don't miss any adventures of the cavemice!

#1 The Stone of Fire

#2 Watch Your Tail!

#3 Help, I'm in Hot Lava!

#4 The Fast and the Frozen

#5 The Great Mouse Race

#6 Don't Wake the Dinosaur!

#7 I'm a Scaredy-Mouse!

Up Next!

#8 Surfing for Secrets

Be sure to read all my fabumouse adventures!

#1 Lost Treasure of the Emerald Eye

#2 The Curse of the Cheese Pyramid

#3 Cat and Mouse in a Haunted House

#4 I'm Too Fond of My Fur!

#5 Four Mice Deep in the Jungle

#6 Paws Off, Cheddarface!

#7 Red Pizzas for a Blue Count

#8 Attack of the Bandit Cats

#9 A Fabumouse Vacation for Geronimo

#10 All Because of a Cup of Coffee

#11 It's Halloween, You 'Fraidy Mouse!

#12 Merry Christmas, Geronimo!

#13 The Phantom of the Subway

#14 The Temple of the Ruby of Fire

#15 The Mona Mousa Code

#16 A Cheese-Colored Camper

#17 Watch Your Whiskers, Stilton!

#18 Shipwreck on the Pirate Islands

#19 My Name Is Stilton, Geronimo Stilton

#20 Surf's Up, Geronimo!

#21 The Wild, Wild West

#22 The Secret of Cacklefur Castle

A Christmas Tale

#23 Valentine's Day Disaster

#24 Field Trip to Niagara Falls

#25 The Search for Sunken Treasure

#26 The Mummy with No Name

#27 The Christmas Toy Factory

#28 Wedding Crasher

#29 Down and Out Down Under

#30 The Mouse Island Marathon

#31 The Mysterious Cheese Thief

Christmas Catastrophe

#32 Valley of the Giant Skeletons

#33 Geronimo and the Gold Medal Mystery

#34 Geronimo Stilton, Secret Agent

#35 A Very Merry Christmas

#36 Geronimo's Valentine

#37 The Race Across America

#38 A Fabumouse School Adventure

#39 Singing Sensation

#40 The Karate Mouse

#41 Mighty Mount Kilimanjaro

#42 The Peculiar Pumpkin Thief

#43 I'm Not a Supermouse!

#44 The Giant Diamond Robbery

#45 Save the White Whale!

#46 The Haunted Castle

#47 Run for the Hills, Geronimo!

#48 The Mystery in Venice

#49 The Way of the Samurai

#50 This Hotel Is Haunted!

#51 The Enormouse Pearl Heist

#52 Mouse in Space!

#53 Rumble in the Jungle

#54 Get into Gear, Stilton!

#55 The Golden Statue Plot

#56 Flight of the Red Bandit

The Hunt for the Golden Book

#57 The Stinky Cheese Vacation

#58 The Super Chef Contest

#59 Welcome to Moldy Manor

The Hunt for the Curious Cheese

#60 The Treasure of Easter Island

Don't miss my journeys through time!

MEET
GERONIMO STILTONIX

He is a spacemouse — the Geronimo Stilton of a parallel universe! He is captain of the spaceship *MouseStar 1*. While flying through the cosmos, he visits distant planets and meets crazy aliens. His adventures are out of this world!

#1 Alien Escape

#2 You're Mine, Captain!

#3 Ice Planet Adventure

#4 The Galactic Goal

Don't miss these exciting Thea Sisters adventures!

Thea Stilton and the
Dragon's Code

Thea Stilton and the
Mountain of Fire

Thea Stilton and the
Ghost of the Shipwreck

Thea Stilton and the
Secret City

Thea Stilton and the
Mystery in Paris

Thea Stilton and the
Cherry Blossom Adventure

Thea Stilton and the
Star Castaways

Thea Stilton: Big Trouble
in the Big Apple

Thea Stilton and the
Ice Treasure

Thea Stilton and the
Secret of the Old Castle

Thea Stilton and the
Blue Scarab Hunt

Thea Stilton and the
Prince's Emerald

Thea Stilton and the Mystery
on the Orient Express

Thea Stilton and the
Dancing Shadows

Thea Stilton and the
Legend of the Fire Flowers

Thea Stilton and the
Spanish Dance Mission

Thea Stilton and the
Journey to the Lion's Den

Thea Stilton and the
Great Tulip Heist

Thea Stilton and the
Chocolate Sabotage

Thea Stilton and the
Missing Myth

Thea Stilton and the
Lost Letters

Old Mouse City
(MOUSE ISLAND)

GOSSIP
RADIO

THE CAVE OF
MEMORIES

THE STONE
GAZETTE

TRAP'S HOUSE

THE ROTTEN
TOOTH TAVERN

LIBERTY
ROCK

UGH UGH
CABIN

DINO
RIVER

CHEDDAR VOLCANO

SINGING ROCK SQUARE

FTYMOUSE HOUSE

HOSPITAL

FLIGHTPORT

SUBWAYSAURUS STATION

GRANDMA RATROCK'S HOUSE

THEA'S HOUSE

THE SHAMAN'S GROTTO

GERONIMO'S HOUSE

DEAR MOUSE FRIENDS,
THANKS FOR READING,
AND GOOD-BYE UNTIL
THE NEXT BOOK!